I'm Sorry

First published in Great Britain by HarperCollins*Publishers* Ltd in 2000
This edition produced for Premier Direct in 2000

1 3 5 7 9 10 8 6 4 2

ISBN: 0 00 760897 7

The HarperCollins website address is: www.**fire**and**water**.com

Printed in Hong Kong.

I'm Sorry

Sam McBratney
illustrated by Jennifer Eachus

Collins
An Imprint of HarperCollinsPublishers

I have a friend I love the best.

I have a friend I love the best.

She plays at my house every day,
or else I play at hers.

I have a friend I love the best.
I think she's nice.

The things we do
always make me laugh,
and she thinks I'm nice, too.

She lets me be the teacher
when we teach our
toys to read...

...I let her be the doctor
and fix my bones.

We make her baby smile
when he wakes up
from his sleep...

...And sometimes we put our wellies on

to see how deep the puddles are.

I have a friend I love the best.
I think she's nice.

The things we do
always make me laugh,
and she thinks I'm nice, too.
But...

I SHOUTED at my friend today,

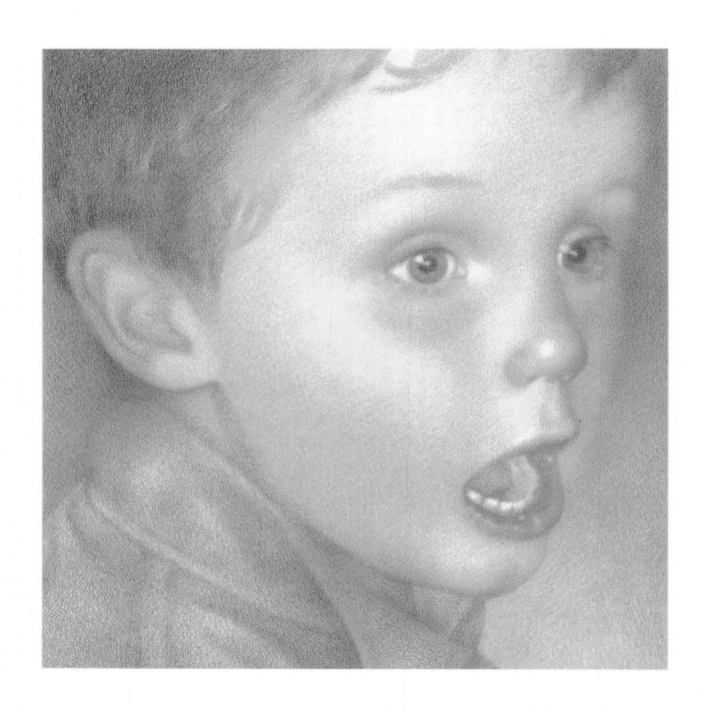

and she shouted back at me.

I wouldn't speak to
her any more, and
she won't speak to me.

My friend shouted at me today,
and I shouted back at her.
She wouldn't play with me any more,
and I won't play with her.

I pretend my friend's not there,

and she pretends she doesn't care, but...

I do care.

If my friend was as sad as I am sad, this is what she would do:

she would come and say, "I'm sorry,"

and I would say sorry, too.